BOOK 2

Maxat
In The Royal Palace

WRITTEN BY AIJAN

Maxat was about to fall asleep as he heard murmurs:

'...Hm...mm... three, four, five, six, seven, eight, nine, ten, eleven counted the little tiger, with his head poking out of the window and looking into the darkness of the night.

'Hey, what you doing?' interrupted Maxat with a yawn.

'Counting the stars in the sky... fourteen, fifteen, sixteen, seventeen...'

'Ah-ha-ha-ha-ha, silly little tiger! But there are billions of stars out there, ha-ha' laughed the boy turning on his side to get more comfortable ready to sleep.

'OH! I know. Let's go out on the veranda, and I'll show you I can do it.' Ermek dragged Maxat out of the bedroom. 'Heyyy... Come!'

'Ahh,..oh, well,' said the boy, lazily following the tiger cub. 'Some fresh air before bed would do us good, I suppose.'

The garden smelt of roses. The summer night breeze and lulling cricket led the pair to their favourite hammock, where the little magician laid cozily snuggled up with his fluffy friend.

'Now, you can count your stars, tiger baby,' he said, yawning, 'and let me know in the morning how it went.'

'Oh,... my stars, it's breathtaking...' said an amazed Ermek. 'I'm afraid a thousand nights won't be enough to count all of them!'

'Told ya. Our Universe is so huge. Sleep!'

'Ah, then I'll count only the brightest ones.'

'They are the closest to us, so try,' said the magician, smiling.

'And don't forget the one closest to you, Ermek, - Maxat the Magician.'

The dead of night was broken by the flap of wings and a familiar warm voice. 'Surely, he IS OUR STAR.'

Ermek hopped out of the hammock in wonder.

'Kairat, what a surprise to see you!' exclaimed Maxat. He stretched out his arm for the golden falcon to sit on.

'My friends, I've got an invitation from our Queen Aijan, for You to perform a magic show for her daughters, Princesses Pariza and Medina.

'Really? I wonder why. I've heard that Princess Pariza is poorly.'

'Oh, Maxat, remember the talent show last year? The two princesses sang and danced as a duo,' said an excited Ermek.

'Of course, and they were a huge success, especially Pariza - she danced so beautifully,' said Maxat.

'And Medina, her voice was amazing, pure, like a nightingale,' added Ermek.

'But... we've not heard of them since then. What happened, Kairat? You, surely, know more than we do, don't you?'

'Well... Indeed, the princesses are very talented and creative. They were raised to love the arts which they practised and performed.' Kairat then told their story.

They are twins. Medina loves singing and Pariza loved to dance, that's how you'd know the difference between them. The palace was always busy with concerts, parties, and amusements. And so it was...

Until... one winter day the princesses went sledging in the mountains. They enjoyed the soft snow sparkling in the sunshine. They slid down the mountains with other children, giggling and shrieking in delight.

Then Pariza chose a steep slope and slid too fast. She crashed right into a ditch, before she realized how dangerous her course was. Her legs were trapped under heavy snow and she felt a sharp pain in her back.

Others hurried to dig her out, and they carried her home before sunset. When she awoke the next morning, Pariza, to her horror, was unable to walk.

All the best doctors of Jardi-Su tried to help, but the girl could never stand on her feet again. The Queen was distraught. She became very sad since then, and nothing could make her smile.

But this morning, when I saw her sitting by Pariza's bedside, full of sorrow, something dawned upon me, and I thought of you, Maxat.

'Of me?..'

'Yes. I believe You can cheer up the Queen and the princesses. And so I told the Queen: "The young magician is very popular with the children of Jardi-Su; his shows are nothing less than wonderful!"

"I've heard of him,.. but, how can he possibly...?" she said.

"Ah, Mother, I'd love to see him. Can I? Can I?" begged Medina, clapping and jumping. "Plea-eese!"

"He's got a little tiger, who helps him do his shows," quietly added Pariza.

"Well, I suppose it could be fun!" agreed Her Majesty.

'So here I am. As you know, I'm the Queen's trusted advisor, she listens to me. May I count on you guys?' asked the proud falcon as he hopped onto the veranda fence in front of them.

'Why not!' exclaimed the little tiger, who was ready for action.

'Oh, WOW!...I'd gladly meet our Queen and the princesses, but.., err...' stunned, Maxat paused, looking at them both.

'They'd be soo-ooo happy, Maxat,' said Kairat.

'Ah, all right.' The magician stood up decidedly rubbing his palms together. 'Ermek, we'd better get ready for a show the Royal Palace will long remember!'

'That's my boy! I knew you wouldn't let me down. Now, rest. Tomorrow is a big day.' With that, Kairat flew away into the darkness.

Maxat and Ermek discussed the scenario for the Royal show. They rehearsed their magic tricks, even though it was a late hour. Soon Ermek fell blissfully asleep. Maxat was too excited to sleep at first, but a soft breezy night air soon lulled him into a deep sleep.

They both woke up early and rehearsed their important performance over and over again.

'Ah, if only we had one more day Ermek, we'd make it flawless.' The boy felt a little weary.

'Well, Her Majesty's wish is our command. We shall do our best,' reassured Ermek, gobbling his breakfast. 'Come and eat, master. Relax.'

Everything in the Royal Palace was ready for a magic show.
The servants bustled about; the butlers welcomed the guests. Huge crystal chandeliers and garlands of colourful lights illuminated fine mosaics on high windows, beautiful sculptures and fresh flower arrangements.

Now all gathered in the large concert hall, young children buzzed with excitement. Then a loud bell rang with an announcement:

'HER ROYAL MAJESTY THE QUEEN!'

The crowned lady walked with a regal gait onto the Royal balcony. She was followed by the princesses, their governesses and two guards. Queen Aijan was petite, in a glittering dress, topped with a long blue cloak embroidered with diamonds.

The princesses wore colourful hats and beautiful dresses. Pariza though, looked rather pale, unlike her sister, whose excitement showed in her rosy cheeks.

Everyone stood up and bowed to the Royal family. Then the lights dimmed and went off.

'LADIES AND GENTLEMEN. BOYS AND GIRLS. ARE YOU READY FOR A SHOW?' asked Kairat's voice.

'YES!!', the crowd shouted.

'THEN, WELCOME TO THE WORLD OF MAGIC...' There was cheerful music while the spotlight fell on the right-hand corner of the stage. The jolly tiger cub appeared in a moment, skillfully juggling several strawberries. He walked back and forth, continuing his amusing trick. At last, he tossed the berries, which lined up vertically to fall right into his mouth, one after another, WOWEEE-EEEl!

The funny juggler, with a full mouth, gave himself time to chew and eat them as the audience burst into laughter. Ermek jumped and made a magnificent backflip, which received cheers and applause.

The stripy little performer bowed proudly, then put a finger to his lips, inviting everyone to calm down as rumbling music played amidst the darkness. A mystical figure in a cloak appeared in the middle of the stage. Suddenly it made a full circle around itself and with one graceful move of the arm threw the cloak off. And there HE WAS, in all his glory!

'THE STAR YOU'VE ALL BEEN WAITING FOR, - MAXAT THE MAGICIAN!!' announced Ermek. Maxat took his Magic Hat off and waved his wand over it. Beautiful bouquets of wild red roses magically grew from inside the hat, then Ermek proudly presented them to Her Majesty and the princesses.

The princesses laughed and clapped in delight.

'Ah, they smell lovely,' said Queen Aijan, and smiled.

'They are from our beautiful mountains, my Queen,' said Ermek. He bowed, then disappeared behind the stage curtain. As cheerful music played, plenty of colourful balloons descended magically onto the people. The children wowed and laughed, tossing them to each other.

'Maxat, look over there!' shouted Medina, pointing at a blue balloon that was trapped on a chandelier. Maxat flew right up there.

'AH, THAT'S THE ONE I'M LOOKING FOR!.. Come here, my dear, GOTCHA!' he said to the escaped balloon as if it was alive. The magician returned to the stage, covered it with his magic shawl, waved his Magic Wand and said: 'CASTA-MA-DINAMAS.' He shook the shawl, holding the audience's watchful gaze, and slowly lifted it up. Then, suddenly out came... you wouldn't believe it...

...ERMEK!

The boisterous tiger was met with laughter and applause from the surprised spectators. He held a little mystery box. With one magical tiger leap he reached out to the Royal balcony and delivered it to the little princess in the wheelchair.

'Please open it, my Princess,' he urged her. Curious, Pariza unlocked the enchanting trinket box. Then everyone could hear beautiful soft music coming out of it, as a lovely figurine of a princess danced to that fairy sound. A huge colourful hologram of her instantly appeared in the air for all to see.

'Ahhh,..' the audience sighed. The dancing figurine looked amazing and melted everyone's hearts.

Pariza held it to her heart and closed her eyes. In her great desire to dance she almost stood up, following the magic music, but a sudden voice in her head said: 'I can't walk.'

She fell awkwardly back on her chair, bursting into tears.

'Oh, my darling girl, SH...shsh, it's all right,' said her mother, who cuddled her and stroked the girl's cheeks. There was an uneasy moment. The Queen, the princesses, as well as their governesses, looked worried while comforting Pariza.

Maxat had to do something. There's so much at stake! God knows what will happen if he fails the show. His good name may suffer and would possibly never be restored again.

He paused nervously, as Kairat reached out to him and whispered:

'Don't despair, my little friend, I think you should use your knowledge from your ancient books. Try and concentrate.'

'Perhaps, I should try THE POWER OF WORDS...' said the boy.

'YES, plus your magic. It will work!' agreed Ermek with confidence.

'Take this golden feather of mine. It will help you too. Now, go on, amaze them! All is well.' reassured Kairat.
The grateful magician attached the feather to his Magic Hat.

The falcon, meanwhile, flew to the Queen and said:

'I beg your indulgence, my Queen, the boy is practically an orphan, with an unusual family history and...'

'An orphan? Really?..' interrupted the Queen. There was tension in the air. She looked at Maxat for a moment, then commanded: «Continue!»

The audience waited, wondering what the young magician was going to show next.

Maxat took a moment to compose himself. Then, suddenly the hall was filled with a magnificent magic sparkle. Princess Pariza was lit up with a bright light. Her dress and shoes were magically transformed into a beautiful dancing outfit.

'WOWW, WONDERFUL!' cheered the dazzled audience.

Pariza couldn't believe her eyes. Maxat then flew right to her, lifted her and they flew up landing gracefully on the stage. Everyone's eyes were glued on them.

'Now, your highness, you may stand up and do what your heart loves the most - DANCE!' said Maxat, who almost sounded like an angel.

'But... Maxat, have you forgotten I can't walk?' whimpered Pariza. 'Oops, hold me dear, I'll fall!'

'Yes, you can. YOU CAN, JUST BELIEVE IN MIRACLES, MY PRINCESS. THE MAGIC IS HAPPENING, RIGHT NOW,' he smiled at her.

'You can do it, young lady!' someone shouted.

'YE-ES!' cheered the rest of the audience.

'Remember how happy you were when you danced, little princess,' Kairat encouraged her.

'Here's a seven-coloured crystal necklace for you, from your angels, beautiful princess.' said Ermek, carefully placing the prize around her neck. 'IT HAS A MAGIC POWER.' he promised, smiling from ear to ear.

'Ah, thank you my fluffy,' said Pariza. Her face was illuminated by the crystals she wore.
'Go on, little sister you've got nothing to lose! You can do it!' cried Medina from the balcony. 'Your Royal Highnesses, my friends, why don't we help out our Princess?' offered Maxat, 'With our hands put together, well-wishing thoughts, on the count of three let's all say: 'CASTA-MA-DINAMAS'

The Royal court and everyone rose up holding each other's hands.
'READY?.. ONE, TWO, THREE!'
'CASTA-MA-DINAMAS!!' chorused all.
The atmosphere was hypnotic. People looked like they were under a magic spell.
With a huge effort Pariza, being supported by Maxat and Ermek, stood up, made three weary steps forward. Then she walked herself, ALONE! WOWW!! Everybody gasped and watched her in awe.
'I can feel my legs, I can walk! I'm walking!' she cried in disbelief. Her favourite Dance of the Sugar Plum Fairy from Tchaikovsky's ballet 'The Nutcracker' played as she danced beautifully. She was blown away, it was her dream come true!

The restored young ballerina's performance was amazing. With huge excitement and healthy crimson on her cheeks now, she excelled herself in her beautiful skill.

The palace was shaken with the rapturous applause and chanting of the thrilled spectators: 'PA-RI-ZA, PA-RI-ZA, PA-RI-ZA! YEEE-EEEY... MA-XAT, MA-XAT, MA-XAT! BRAVOOO-OOOO!!!'

'Look how many stars we've got tonight! BRAVO!' praised Kairat.
'Ah, baby sister, I'm so proud of you!' cried Medina hugging her twin. Pariza's eyes glistened with happiness. Maxat was all emotional himself. As for Queen Aijan, she couldn't help herself but cried tears of joy.
'You gave us a miracle, Maxat the Magician, for that I shall reward you with whatever you wish for,' said the Queen.

'Your smile and your daughters' happiness is my best reward, Your Majesty,' Maxat humbly replied.

No one had seen such a show before. Queen Aijan glowed with joy and pride, and her palace was a happy place again, with dancing and singing princesses. Her Majesty generously rewarded Maxat with the title of The Royal Magician, and the fastest, most magnificent white stallion in her realm. Maxat named him Ulash.

'WHAT A DAY!' said Maxat and flopped in his hammock, tired.

'Home, sweet home,' cooed Ermek, making himself comfortable on his tiger cub bed on the floor.

'I think I will sleep all night and all day tomorrow,' Maxat yawned.

'Well, the stars need plenty of rest.' said Ermek, 'it's cool, how you managed to hypnotize them all, ha-ha, you are a true star after all!'

'Well, you are a star yourself, that's why you see it in me. And even Pariza, she was awesome, wasn't she, surely a star!
Come, my dear fluffy kitten, I'll show you some constellations.'

'Meow...' said Ermek playfully and he rubbed his fluffy cheek against the boy's feet, showing his love and loyalty.

'Look over there - there's the Big Bear...'
They snuggled up and fell asleep dreaming of the stars.

TO BE CONTINUED

Illustrated by Duc Tran

Republished in United Kingdom 2021
by Eastern Treasure Publishing

ISBN 978-1-291-68858-0

Not long after, Felicity entered the ward for the wedding ceremony, followed by Kitty.

The guests all smiled and sobbed as Felicity walked up the aisle between the beds towards the vicar.

Dr Matthews was best dog so he stood next to Bruce.

'Still got the ring?' joked Bruce.

'Of course,' said Dr Matthews, putting a paw into his pocket. 'Gosh! Where's it gone?' he yelped, and quickly slipped out of the ward.

'I know you've got it,' Dr Matthews held up Maxwell's x-ray, which showed the ring inside Maxwell's beak. 'Open up!' Maxwell shook his head, then jumped out of bed. Dr Matthews chased him down the ward, and out of the doors. Just then, Clare and Arthur were wheeling the cake trolley down the corridor, and that's when Maxwell tripped. The ring shot out of his mouth and buried itself deep in the cake.

'Oh no!' howled Dr Matthews.

Down in the operating theatre Surgeon Sally was preparing to perform a very delicate operation.

'Scalpel,' she ordered.

'Scalpel.' Dr Matthews gave her the scalpel.

'Sugar-tongs.'

'Sugar-tongs.'

With great care, Sally inserted the sugar-tongs into the little cut she'd made in the pink icing. Then, very slowly, she pulled the tongs out again. Clasped in their tip was the ring!

'And with this ring...' the vicar declared,
'I pronounce you... koala and koala.'
  Confetti filled the ward like blossom. Dr Atticus
played the Wedding March, his gas cylinders
hissing tunefully, and the young couple kissed.

The party after was magical: hospital food had never tasted better and, of course, there was the cake. Dr Matthews brought a slice to Sally. 'That was a wonderful operation you performed today, Sally.' he said.

'Oh, an operation's an operation, Matthews. Actually, it was a piece of cake.'

Then it was time for Dr Matthews' speech. He brought out his slip of paper and began. 'Take one pill before meals and one at bedtime...' Oh no! It was Maxwell's prescription. 'And,' he continued quickly, 'I hope you'll be very happy.'

'Hear! Hear!' the staff all cheered.

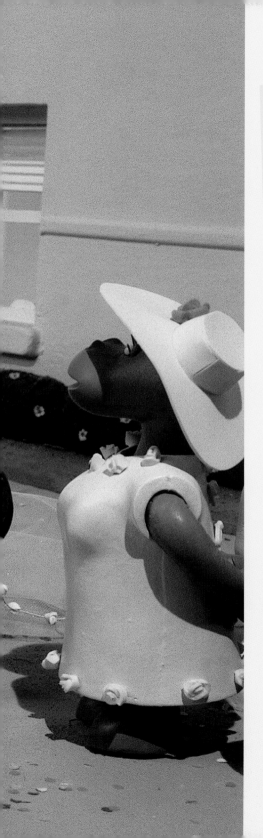

As the bride and groom left the hospital, the Teds started the ambulance helicopter.

'Bye bye, everyone,' the happy couple cried, and Felicity threw the bouquet high into the air. First of all it tumbled towards Kitty. Then the wind from the helicopter blades tossed it towards Dr Matthews, then to Surgeon Sally, whose hat flew off as well.

Finally the bouquet fell in Dr Atticus's paws and Sally's hat fell on his head.

'Oh, I don't think these flowers are meant for me,' said Dr Atticus. 'Would you like them, Sally?'

'Certainly not,' Sally replied, 'but I would like my hat back.'

'Perhaps the bouquet was meant for you, Kitty.' He presented Kitty with the flowers.

'I think it was,' Kitty agreed. 'Don't you, Dr Matthews?'

But Dr Matthews didn't like to say.